STAR WARS

Editor - Zachary Rau
Contributing Editor - Dave Schreiber
Graphic Designer and Letterer - Monalisa J. de Asis
Cover Designer - Gary Shum

Production Managers - Jennifer Miller and Mutsumi Miyazaki
Senior Designer - Anna Kernbaum
Senior Editor - Elizabeth Hurchalla
Managing Editor - Lindsey Johnston
VP of Production - Ron Klamert
Publisher & Editor in Chief - Mike Kiley
President & C.O.O. - John Parker
C.E.O. - Stuart Levy

E-mail: info@TOKYOPOP.com
Come visit us online at www.TOKYOPOP.com
Visit the official Star Wars website at www.starwars.com

A ⓒTOKYOPOP® Cine-Manga® Book
TOKYOPOP Inc.
5900 Wilshire Blvd., Suite 2000
Los Angeles, CA 90036

Star Wars: Attack of the Clones

ISBN: 1-59532-976-5

First TOKYOPOP® printing: November 2005

10 9 8 7 6 5 4 3 2 1

Printed in Italy

STAR WARS

EPISODE II
ATTACK OF THE CLONES

STORY AND SCREENPLAY BY
GEORGE LUCAS

HAMBURG • LONDON • LOS ANGELES • TOKYO

Senator Padmé Amidala:
Senator of Naboo

Anakin Skywalker:
Obi-Wan's apprentice

Obi-Wan Kenobi: Jedi Master and Anakin
Skywalker's teacher and mentor

Yoda: Jedi Master

Senator Palpatine:
Supreme Chancellor
of the Republic

Nute Gunray:
Viceroy of the
Trade Federation

Jango Fett and
Boba Fett: The
bounty hunter
and his son

Count Dooku:
Leader of the
Separatists

A long time ago in a galaxy far, far away....

There is unrest in the Galactic Senate.
Several thousand solar systems have declared
their intentions to leave the Republic.

This separatist movement,
under the leadership of Count Dooku,
has made it difficult for the limited
number of Jedi Knights to maintain peace
and order in the galaxy.

Senator Amidala, the former Queen of
Naboo, is returning to the Galactic Senate
to vote on the critical issue of creating
an ARMY OF THE REPUBLIC to
assist the overwhelmed Jedi....

LATER, THE JEDI COUNCIL MEETS WITH CHANCELLOR PALPATINE.

I don't know how much longer I can hold off the vote, my friends. More and more star systems are joining the Separatists. I will not let this Republic be split in two. My negotiations will not fail!

If they do, you must realize there aren't enough Jedi to protect the Republic. We are keepers of the peace, not soldiers.

Master Yoda, do you really think it will come to war?

The dark side clouds everything. Impossible to see, the future is. But this I am sure of...do their duty, the Jedi will.

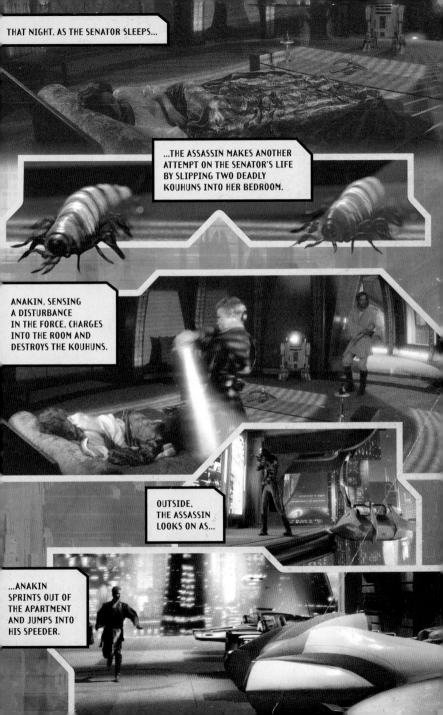

MEANWHILE, BACK ON NABOO, ANAKIN AND PADMÉ HAVE ARRIVED AT THE LAKE HIDEAWAY...

We used to come here for school retreats. We would swim to that island over there every day. I love the water.

I do too. I guess it comes from growing up on a desert planet.

We used to lie on the sand and let the sun dry us...and try to guess the names of the birds singing.

I don't like sand. It's coarse and rough. Not like here. Here everything is soft... and smooth.

There was an old man here who made magical glass out of sand...

Here, everything is magical.

You could look into the glass and see the water. It looked so real, but it wasn't...

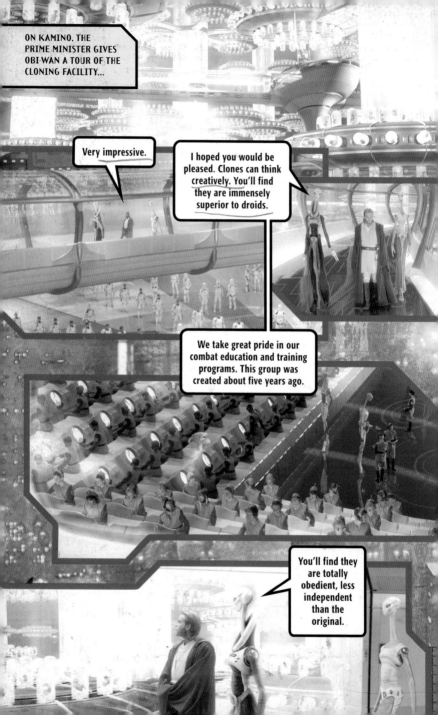

OUTSIDE OF THE CITY OF KAMINO ON A LANDING PLATFORM, OBI-WAN IS FINDING IT MUCH MORE DIFFICULT TO CAPTURE JANGO FETT THAN HE'D THOUGHT.

THE BOUNTY HUNTER LAUNCHES INTO THE AIR WITH HIS ROCKETPACK...

...AND NEARLY HITS OBI-WAN WITH A LASER BLAST.

JANGO FETT
CHARGES HIM...
...BUT OBI-WAN IS READY,
FLIPPING IN THE AIR AND
KICKING JANGO FETT...
...KNOCKING OFF
HIS ROCKETPACK!
JANGO FETT RESPONDS BY
SHOOTING A THIN WIRE FROM
HIS WRISTPACK...
...SNARING THE JEDI.

IN THE PROCESS, JANGO FETT LOSES HIS BALANCE AND SLIDES DOWN THE SIDE OF THE PLATFORM...

...PULLING OBI-WAN WITH HIM, WHO SLIDES PAST HIM AND OFF THE PLATFORM...

...GIVING JANGO FETT ONLY SECONDS TO KEEP HIMSELF FROM GETTING PULLED OVER THE EDGE...

...LEAVING OBI-WAN DANGLING PRECARIOUSLY ABOVE THE RAGING OCEAN.

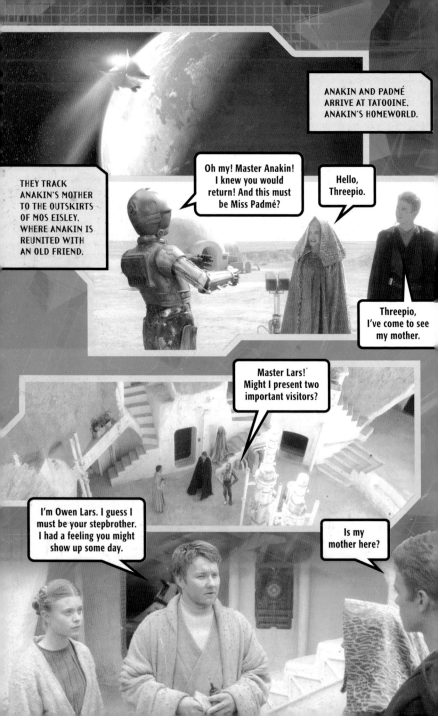

THAT NIGHT, THE YOUNG JEDI SPEEDS ACROSS THE DESERT...

...PICKING UP CLUES, TRACKING THE TUSKEN RAIDERS...

...SEARCHING FOR HIS MOTHER.

OBI-WAN BARELY ESCAPES THE SHOCK WAVE AS THE ASTEROIDS AROUND THE JEDI'S SHIP EXPLODE.

BUT THE BOUNTY HUNTER IS PERSISTENT.

THINKING FAST, OBI-WAN EJECTS HIS SPARE PARTS CANISTERS...

...FOOLING THE BOUNTY HUNTER'S SENSORS AS HE HIDES HIS STAR FIGHTER BEHIND A LARGE ASTEROID.

WAITING UNTIL IT'S CLEAR, OBI-WAN LEAVES THE ASTEROID FIELD AND FOLLOWS JANGO FETT DOWN TO THE SURFACE OF THE PLANET GEONOSIS.

There's an unusual concentration of Federation ships over there, Arfour.

OBI-WAN QUIETLY MAKES HIS WAY TO THE TOP OF A RIDGE...

...AND SPIES JANGO FETT LANDING NEAR A FEDERATION SHIP.

43

OBI-WAN TRACKS THE BOUNTY HUNTER INTO THE CATACOMBS OF GEONOSIS, WHERE HE FINDS A MASSIVE DROID FACTORY.

Now, we must persuade the Commerce Guild and the Corporate Alliance to sign the treaty.

What about the Senator from Naboo? Is she dead yet? I'm not signing your treaty until I have her head on my desk.

AS OBI-WAN SEARCHES THE CATACOMBS, HE STUMBLES UPON A SECRET CONVERSATION COUNT DOOKU IS HAVING WITH VICEROY GUNRAY AND ARCHDUKE POGGLE.

I am a man of my word.

<With these new battle droids we've built for you, Viceroy, you'll have the finest army in the galaxy.>

...AND FOLLOWS THE VOICES TO A CONFERENCE ROOM...

44

ANAKIN BURSTS OUT OF THE HUT AND CUTS DOWN TWO TUSKEN RAIDERS.

THE RAIDERS CHARGE THE VENGEFUL JEDI...

...HEADING STRAIGHT TO THEIR SLAUGHTER.

UNAWARE OF OBI-WAN'S MESSAGE, ANAKIN RETURNS HIS MOTHER TO HER HOME.

I couldn't save her... Why did she have to die? Why couldn't I save her?

Sometimes there are things no one can fix. You're not all-powerful, Annie.

Annie, what is it? There's something more, isn't there?

I...I killed them all. And not just the men, but the women and children too. I slaughtered them like animals! I couldn't control myself. I don't want to hate them, but I just can't forgive them.

AFTER THE FUNERAL, ANAKIN AND PADMÉ DISCOVER OBI-WAN'S MESSAGE AND RELAY IT TO CORUSCANT...

I tracked the bounty hunter to the droid foundries on Geonosis. The Trade Federation is to take delivery of a droid army here.

It is clear that Viceroy Gunray is behind the assassination attempts on Senator Amidala. The Commerce Guilds and Corporate Alliance have both pledged their armies to Count Dooku and are forming an...

Wait! Wait!

OBI-WAN'S MESSAGE SPUTTERS, THEN STOPS!

More happening on Geonosis, I feel, than has been revealed.

52

...THE HUGE UNDERGROUND DROID FOUNDRIES.

WHEN PADMÉ JUMPS ONTO A CONVEYOR BELT, ANAKIN LEAPS AFTER HER.

Padmé!

PADMÉ DESPERATELY TRIES TO AVOID THE AUTOMATED MACHINES...

...AS ANAKIN TRIES TO FOLLOW HER.

ANAKIN AND PADMÉ ARE CARTED INTO THE EXECUTION ARENA, WHERE THOUSANDS OF GEONOSIANS CHEER FOR THEIR IMMINENT DEMISE.

HUGE, DEADLY CREATURES ARE LED INTO THE ARENA AND HERDED STRAIGHT FOR THE CAPTIVES...

...WHILE A FAMILIAR FACE WATCHES FROM THE CROWD.

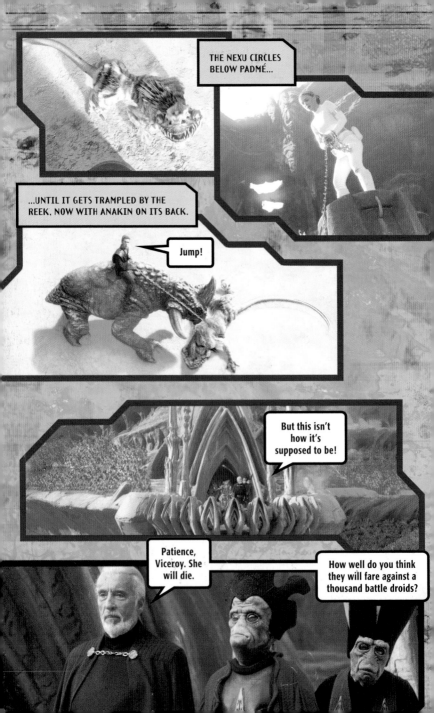

AS DOOKU SPEAKS, BATTLE DROIDS POUR INTO THE EXECUTION ARENA...

..AND SURROUND PADMÉ, ANAKIN AND OBI-WAN.

JUST AS THE BATTLE DROIDS TAKE UP POSITION AROUND THE ARENA, JEDI KNIGHTS COME STREAMING OUT OF THE ENTRANCE TUNNELS. PABLO JI AND KIT FISTO...

...SHAAK TI AND LUMINARA UNDULI...

...AAYLA SECURA AND KI-ADI-MUNDI...

...COLEMAN TREBOR...

...MACE WINDU AND MANY MORE PREPARE TO FIGHT THE DROID ARMY AND SAVE THE CAPTIVE JEDI.

Sorry to disappoint you, Dooku. This party's over.

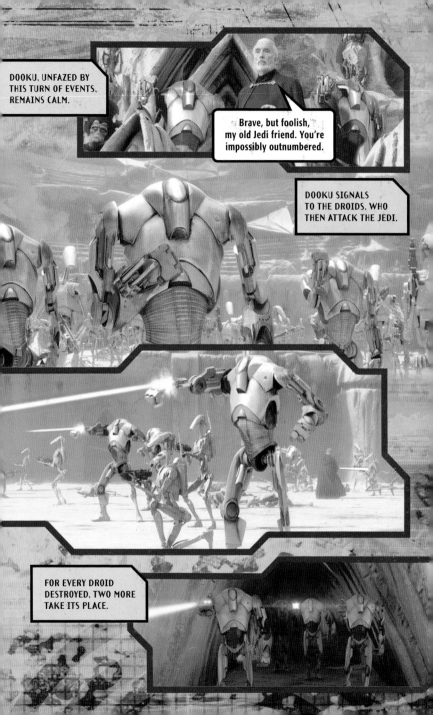

THOUGH SUPER BATTLE DROIDS FIRE RELENTLESSLY, PADMÉ AND THE JEDI FIGHT BACK VALIANTLY.

OBI-WAN AND MACE WINDU JOIN FORCES IN THE CENTER OF THE FRAY...

...DESPERATELY TRYING TO KEEP CONTROL OF THE BATTLE...

...BUT MORE JEDI FALL WITH EVERY PASSING MOMENT.

THE DROID ARMY SURROUNDS WHAT IS
LEFT OF THE OVERWHELMED JEDI...

...THEN SUDDENLY STOP.

ONLY A SMALL NUMBER OF JEDI REMAIN OF THE HUNDREDS THAT BEGAN THE BATTLE.

Master Windu, you have fought gallantly. Worthy of recognition in the archives of the Jedi order. Now it is finished. Surrender, and your lives will be spared.

We will not be hostages for you to barter with, Dooku.

SUDDENLY, FROM HIGH ABOVE, THE ROAR OF ENGINES IS HEARD...

...AS YODA ARRIVES WITH REINFORCEMENTS...

Circle the Jedi. A perimeter create around the survivors.

...AND BEGINS A FULL-SCALE WAR.

AS THE TIDE TURNS AGAINST THE DROID ARMY, DOOKU LOOKS ON IN ANGER BEFORE FLEEING FROM THE ARENA.

MOMENTS LATER, THE GUNSHIPS LAND...

...AND THE LAST OF THE JEDI GET ON BOARD.

WHEN THE ARENA CLEARS, ONLY ONE REMAINS. THOUGH JANGO FETT HAS MET HIS DEMISE, HIS SON LIVES ON.

SOON, THE BATTLE HAS SPREAD FROM THE ARENA TO THE ENTIRE PLANET.

Capture Dooku we must. If escapes he does, rally he will, more systems to his cause.

YODA REACHES THE BATTLE COMMAND CENTER IN TIME TO DIRECT THE CLONE ARMY.

More battalions to the left. Encircle them we must, then divide.

BACK AT THE CLONE ARMY COMMAND CENTER...

CONCENTRATE ALL YOUR FIRE ON THE NEAREST STARSHIP CORE.

DOZENS OF TURBOLASERS BLAST THE FEDERATION CORE...

...BRINGING IT CRASHING TO THE GROUND.

WAVE AFTER WAVE OF CLONE TROOPERS ADVANCE ON THE FEDERATION SHIPS...

BUT JUST AS IT'S ABOUT TO LAND ON THE UNCONSCIOUS JEDI...

...YODA STOPS ITS FALL...

...GIVING DOOKU THE CHANCE TO ESCAPE IN HIS SHIP.

BACK FROM THE DUNES, PADMÉ SHOOTS AT DOOKU'S SHIP AS IT FLIES OFF...

...THEN RUSHES INTO THE HANGAR.

Anakin!

Jedi Starfighter

Small wedge-shaped single-pilot ship used by the Jedi order. A truncated astromech droid is hard-wired into the starfighter's port side, providing repair and navigation information to the Jedi pilot. The vessel is too small to carry a hyperdrive and instead relies on a separate hyperspace transport ring for transit through hyperspace.

Naboo Royal Cruiser

Senator Padmé Amidala's official starship. A majestic craft with smooth lines, an unblemished chromed surface and a bold flying wing silhouette, the Naboo Royal Cruiser is unmistakable in its origins.

Republic Assault Ship

While the Kaminoans labored to perfect an indomitable clone army, the neighboring shipyards of Rothana were subcontracted to develop the hardware, armor and transports for the new infantry. The Republic uses these titan transport vessels to bring clone troopers to the battlefields of Geonosis.

SPHA-T Self-Propelled Heavy Artillery–Turbolaser

An armored juggernaut with incredible firepower, the SPHA-T is a self-propelled laser artillery tank. Rather than relying on a rotating turret, the entire vehicle can reposition itself by means of twelve articulated legs. Considerably larger than the AT-TE walker, the SPHA-T provides long-range surface-to-surface and surface-to-air fire, coordinated by a crack team of clone troopers.

Republic Attack Gunship

Republic Attack Gunships rain down blistering barrages of laser and rocket retribution against the droid forces of the Separatists. Each winged gunship is covered in weapons, offering air-to-surface and air-to-air support as well as serving as an infantry transport.

Vehicles of The Federation

Trade Federation Battleship and Core

At over three kilometers in diameter, these enormous vessels resemble flattened disks with a central sphere containing the ship's bridge and landing core. The disk is broken at the front of the craft, revealing two mammoth docking bays lined with forward docking claws. The reclusive Neimoidian typically seal themselves in the ship's spacious bridge while their legions of droids handle the operation of the mighty craft.

Hailfire Droid

A self-aware mobile missile platform used exclusively by the InterGalactic Banking Clan, hailfire droids deliver surface-to-surface and surface-to-air attacks with their stacked banks of thirty rocket warheads.

Slave I

The elliptical silhouette of the *Slave I* is the last thing any fugitive would want to see on their rear sensor display. The *Slave I*'s sophisticated antidetection gear and stealth package ensure that very few fugitives ever see their captor coming. The vessel is armed with numerous laser cannons, as well as concealed projectile launchers and a seismic charge deployer.

Zam Wesell's Airspeeder

During her mission to assassinate Senator Padmé Amidala on Coruscant, bounty hunter Zam Wesell employed an ultra-sleek airspeeder model. The wickedly forked green-hued dragster emits a chilling howl as it flies.

Geonosian Solar Sailer

An exotic, alien conveyance befitting Count Dooku's enigmatic character, the Geonosian solar sailer uses unique technology to propel the craft through both realspace and hyperspace. The vessel's carapace opens to expel its diaphanous sail, which unfurls into a parabolic chute that gathers energetic A-particles for propulsion.

TOKYOPOP
STAR WARS
CLONE WARS
The Clone Wars are spreading like a fire across the galaxy!
Now In Stores!
Y
YOUTH AGE 10+
CINE-MANGA
www.TOKYOPOP.com
TM or ® & © 2005 Lucasfilm Ltd. Title and character and place names protected by all applicable trademark laws. All Rights Reserved. Used Under Authorization.